Chuckie tugged at Tommy's sleeve. "Did you hear that?" he yelled over the noise of the crowd. "That man just said your daddy is going into the ring with the big meanie!"

"He's gonna get pureed," added Kimi. "That means smooshed up like an eggplant."

"Oh, Tommy, he's doomed, doomed!" wailed Chuckie.

"No, he's not," said Tommy. "'Cause we're gonna save him. I gots an idea!"

"I was afraid you were gonna say that," gulped Chuckie.

Rugrats Chapter Books

Rugrats in the Ring

It was a dark and stormy night...

...outside the library of
LARRY GRESS

©UFS

Based on the TV series *Rugrats*® created by Arlene Klasky, Gabor Csupo,
and Paul Germain as seen on Nickelodeon®

ISBN 0-439-40207-7

12 11 10 9 8 7 6 5 4 3 2 1   2 3 4 5 6 7/0

Printed in the U.S.A.
First Scholastic printing, January 2002

Rugrats in the Ring

by Sarah Willson
illustrated by BKN Studios

SCHOLASTIC INC.

New York Toronto London Auckland Sydney
Mexico City New Delhi Hong Kong Buenos Aires

Chapter 1

"Driving this car is the most funnest thing in the whole wild world!" said Chuckie. He turned the steering wheel to the left, then swung it back to the right. "Wheeeee!" he cried, giggling.

"Chuckie, it would be even funnerer if we went somewheres," said Kimi, who was sitting next to him in the passenger seat of the red toy car. "It's opposed to make noise and bump up and down."

"I like it fine just like this," said Chuckie. "I like just about everything at Buck E. Bee's restaurant. 'Cept when they show scary stuff on the TBs."

"Look! There's Reptar!" said Lil. She was standing next to Phil in front of a wall of television screens. They watched as twenty-five Reptars appeared on twenty-five television screens.

"Look at all those Reptars!" said Phil in amazement. "I wish we had this many TVs in *our* living room!"

Tommy was sitting waist-deep in colorful plastic balls nearby. "Yeah, Buck E. Bee's is my favoritest place," he agreed. He looked around the crowded restaurant. The huge play area was surrounded by tables where parents sat to keep an eye on their kids while eating dinner. Some of the kids were crawling through the maze of plastic tunnels in the climbing area. A few older ones banged away on the arcade machines that blinked with neon lights. But the largest group of kids could be found in the same area as Phil and Lil—in front of the wall of televisions.

Suddenly twenty-five Dactars appeared on the screens in towering close-up. All the kids gasped at once.

"Oh, no! I knew it!" moaned Chuckie, slipping below the dashboard of the car to hide.

"Get him, Reptar!" shouted Phil.

Chuckie climbed out of the car and buried himself in the ball pit.

Tommy joined his friends in front of the televisions. "Don't worry, Chuckie. Dactar went away," called Tommy over his shoulder.

Chuckie poked his head up.

"Awww, isn't that cute?" said Chas, who sat at a table with the grown-ups nearby. "Chuckie's playing peekaboo in the ball pit."

"This place is great!" said Stu, leaning back in his chair. "We can eat in peace while the kids have a ball!"

"Well, the food isn't bad," said Didi, toying with her decaf-coffee-flavored, rain forest friendly, nonfat frozen yogurt. "But I don't know how much meaningful play interaction goes on here. Most of the kids seem to be watching TV."

Just then a commercial came on. All twenty-five television screens flashed at once.

"It's live! It's huge! It's THE MATCH OF THE CENTURY!" boomed the announcer. "*What* am I *talking* about?" he continued, his voice rising shrilly. "I'm talking about the big *match-up* between the champion,

Bonebreak Jake, and The Duuuuuude!"

Two very large, very muscular men stepped into the picture, their images filling the wall of televisions. One man had long blond hair pulled back into a ponytail. He wore a tiny leopard-print wrap around his waist, and shiny black knee-high boots. He looked into the camera and pounded his fist into the palm of his open hand. The other man was completely bald with a bushy black mustache. He wore a leather vest, and briefs patterned like an American flag. He looked as though he had just taken a swig of some milk gone bad.

"Oh, dear. They're running a *wrestling* commercial during children's programs!" said Didi, shaking her head. "Exposure to this sort of content could cause developmental trauma in a young child!"

Kira nodded. "I couldn't agree more."

"Aw, the kids have no idea what it's all about," said Stu. "Besides, professional wrestling is just harmless entertainment."

"I'm not so sure it's entirely *harmless*," said Chas. "One of those fellas just clocked the other one over the head!"

"Pshaw!" clucked Betty. "Lighten up, guys, pro wrestling is a blast. I never miss a match!" She turned to get a better look. "This is entertainment, American-style!"

Didi sighed and shook her head.

Meanwhile, Chuckie had joined his friends in front of the televisions.

"Tommy?" said Chuckie. "Why are those two growed-ups so mad and growly at each other?"

"I don't know, Chuckie," said Tommy.

"And why is that man dressed in diapies and booties like a baby?" Kimi wanted to know.

"It looks like a bather suit," said Phil.

"Maybe they're going swimmin'," suggested Lil. "'Cept there's no water."

"I'm just glad those big meanies are safe and sound inside those TBs," said Chuckie. "Nobody better throw a ball up there and break one, 'cause I want them to stay in there and not come out here and bother us."

Chapter 2

"Oh, dear, maybe this isn't such a good idea," said Didi worriedly. It was the next morning. "Stu, are you *sure* you'll remember all the instructions I gave you?" She and Betty and Kira were standing near the front door, their overnight bags packed. "I feel so guilty leaving the kids for the night," Didi added.

"Me too," said Kira, looking over at

Chuckie and Kimi, who were happily playing in the playpen. "Maybe we shouldn't go to this Lipschitz mothering retreat."

"Now, now," said Chas, coming over and putting an arm around Kira. "Don't you worry, honey."

"That's right, Deed," said Stu. "We've got everything under control. What could possibly happen?"

Just then Dil threw his rattle, and it hit Stu in the head.

Didi cringed.

"I say we go for it," said Betty.

"We'll take great care of the kids!" Howard assured them.

Didi opened up the brochure she had been holding and looked down at it wistfully. "Well, I *was* really looking forward to Dr. Lipschitz's talk entitled 'It's Not All Your Fault,'" she admitted.

Betty plucked the brochure out of Didi's hand. "'Why Your Baby Ought to Know Physics by Now,'" she read and rolled her eyes.

"I hear his talk, 'Your Child's Slippery Slope to Reform School' is very instructive," said Kira.

"Go on, have a nice time!" said Stu encouragingly.

The moms gave the babies one last hug and kiss and picked up their bags.

"We'll see you tomorrow morning!" called Didi as she headed out. "Make sure the kids don't watch too much TV!"

After the moms had left, Stu picked up the TV remote. He pressed the button, but nothing happened. He peered closely at it. He shook it up and down, then held it up to his ear. "What's the matter with this darn thing?" he muttered. He tried it again, and this time the TV went on.

Chas sat down on the couch next to Howard and Grandpa Lou. "Say!" he said. "It's my favorite program—*This Old Heap!* This is an exciting episode. They're resurfacing tired old countertops!"

The TV crackled with static. Stu banged the remote against his hand, and the TV went off.

"In *my* day we stood up and *walked* to the television set to work the controls!" said Grandpa Lou. "And that was before televisions were even invented!" He shrugged. "I sure as blazes don't care if ya get the thing working. It's not good for ya anyway. In my day we read *books* instead!" He turned toward Stu impatiently. "Did you try banging it? That sometimes works."

Stu banged the clicker on the table, then pointed it at the TV and pressed the button. The television came on again. "There we go!" he cried. A wrestling match was just beginning.

The babies stopped what they were doing and began watching the television too.

"Gee, Stu, I don't know about this," said Chas, glancing over at the babies in their playpen. "Maybe Didi is right. The kids probably should not be exposed to this kind of stuff. It could send the wrong message about conflict resolution."

"Pipe down, Finster. This is great stuff!" said Grandpa Lou, his eyes wide. "Anyway, those sprouts are too busy playing to pay any attention."

"That's right, Dad," said Stu without taking his eyes off the television. "They're way too young to understand what's going on. Hey, look! Here comes The Dude!"

A cloud of smoke filled the TV screen.

Through the clearing mist a large man in a leopard-print outfit emerged. His hair was pulled back in a yellow ponytail.

Chuckie's eyes widened. "There's that big meanie again!" he cried.

"Look! Another growly guy just climbed into that big playpen," said Kimi. "He did a slumbersault and bounced off the bouncy rope."

"Now he's rolling around and ticklin' the other guy, but the other guy's not laughin'," observed Phil.

"They need to learn how to gets along with each other more better," said Lil.

"Um . . . hey, you guys, look at all that smoke!" said Chuckie.

Sure enough, not only was there smoke on the screen, but smoke was coming out of the back of the TV too.

Pffffffffft!!!!

Fuzzy lines rolled up the screen. Then

it went dark except for a tiny dot of white light in the center of it. The smoke continued to rise from the back of the TV in a thin line, and then it disappeared.

Everyone stared at the dark screen. Stu hopped up and ran into the kitchen. They heard him rummaging around in a drawer, and then he hurried back into the living room holding a screwdriver.

The babies watched as Stu unplugged the TV, unscrewed the back panel, and peered inside at the wiring. "Well, that's that," he sighed. "I've tried fixing this thing a dozen times, inside and out, but it's finally broken for sure."

"The TV got broked," whispered Kimi. "And Tommy's daddy just said what was inside got out."

"Uh-oh," said Chuckie. "The big meanie got out of the TB?" He looked warily around Tommy's living room. "If he gots out, then where did he go?

"Don't worry, Chuckie, he prob'ly stayed inside," said Tommy, but he didn't seem sure.

The fathers sat looking glumly at the broken TV.

"We'll miss the end of the match," said Howard.

"That's too bad," said Chas. "I must admit that I was enjoying it a little."

Suddenly Stu snapped his fingers. "Come on! Let's pack up the kids and head over to Reliance Appliance Giants and get a new TV. If we hurry, we might make it back in time to see the end of the match!"

"You all go ahead," said Grandpa Lou. "I'll stay here while Dil finishes his nap." As soon as the door closed, Grandpa Lou fell fast asleep.

Chapter 3

"Welcome to Reliance Appliance Giants, where reliance is practically our middle name," mumbled a bored security guard standing at the front door. The dads walked in, pushing the babies in their strollers.

"It sure is crowded today," said Stu, trying to see over the heads of all the people.

"It seems like there's some sort of promotional event going on," remarked

Chas. The dads moved in closer to see what was happening.

A large man in a leopard-print outfit and shiny boots was standing on a platform in the center of the store, scowling down at the crowd that had gathered to see him. A big pile of boxes was stacked up next to him. He picked up one of the boxes and autographed it. Then he tossed it into the crowd's waiting arms.

The babies looked up at The Dude, shocked.

Stu stood on his toes and cocked his head to the side to read one of the boxes. "'The Dude's Food Processor,'" he read.

Chas peered through his glasses. "'Food ain't got a chance,'" he read slowly. "Oh, I get it," he said. "That fella's hawking his own product line."

"I wonder how he got from the wrestling arena to this store so fast?"

said Howard. "We were just watching him on TV a half an hour ago."

"It must have been taped ahead of time," replied Stu.

The dads and babies watched The Dude pull a potato from a large basket of vegetables. He snarled at the crowd and then crushed the potato between the palms of his huge, beefy hands. "THAT'S what my processor does to your food! Pulverizes it!" he rumbled at the crowd as small bits of potato tumbled out of his fist.

Chuckie gasped and covered his eyes as The Dude picked up a head of cauliflower.

Stu grinned. "The guy's pretty impressive, isn't he? Come on, kids." He gave Tommy's stroller a push. "The TV section is over there."

Stu, Howard, and Chas strolled the kids over toward the television area, and

parked the strollers in front of a TV that was showing a Reptar cartoon. Then the dads wandered off a little ways, examining the different televisions.

Kimi kept trying to get a glimpse of The Dude.

The crowd took a step backward as The Dude pulled out a large eggplant. "You want to see food get pureed?!" he yelled.

"Pureed?" said Kimi to herself. She watched The Dude smoosh the eggplant to a pulp. "Oh," she said with a shudder.

"Tommy?" asked Chuckie in a tiny voice. "Did you see what I just seed?"

"Yeah, Chuckie," Tommy replied.

"That big meanie is here!" said Chuckie. "Right here in this store!"

"He got outta the TV!" said Phil.

"And got a whole lot biggerer all of a sudden," said Lil.

"I guess he eats a lot of vegibles," said

Tommy, turning around in his stroller to get another look at The Dude, who was toweling eggplant goo off of his hands.

Then Tommy nodded his head slowly as he remembered something. "'Member how my daddy took the back offa our TV and said what was inside went out?" They all nodded.

"The meanie musta climbed out the back!" said Tommy.

"I don't like this one bit," said Chuckie. "It was bad enough when he was inside the TB. Now he's outside, and he's a lot biggerer, and he looks like he's not very nice."

Meanwhile, Stu, Chas, and Howard were examining a huge television set.

"That sure is a big one," marveled Chas. "It would take up most of your living room!"

"It looks expensive," said Howard. He

turned over the price tag that hung from the set. "'Fell-Off-a-Truck Sale!'" he read. "Say! That's not a bad price at all!"

"Give me a hand, would you?" asked Stu.

The three dads picked up the TV and staggered to the checkout counter. It was crowded with people buying food processors, but the line moved quickly. They had just managed to heave the huge television onto the counter when suddenly a spotlight shone down on them. Bells rang. Whistles blew. Sirens wailed. Confetti poured down from the ceiling. Even The Dude looked up from his platform where he was karate-chopping coconuts in half with his bare hands.

"Wha-What?" said Stu, looking around in surprise.

The store manager raced over to them.

"Gentlemen!" he bellowed, his white

teeth flashing in the glare of the lights. "Which of you plans to buy this TV set?"

Chas and Howard quickly took a step backward and pointed a finger toward Stu.

"With the purchase of this TV, you are Reliance Appliance Giants' one millionth customer!"

Everyone in line began clapping and cheering.

"As the grand-prize winner, you have won your very own The Dude's Food Processor! But that's not all! You and two of your guests will have VIP seats to the wrestling tournament this evening! A limousine will pick you up and bring you to the arena, where you'll enjoy front-row seats! Then you will join The Dude in the ring for AN APPEARANCE ON LIVE TV!"

"No kidding!" said Stu. "D-D-Do I have to *wrestle* him?" he stammered. He looked over at The Dude, who was curling two crates full of turnips.

The manager chuckled. "Oh no, sir! It's just a publicity appearance for the store. You'll even get to ride in the victory parade!"

Kimi gasped. "He's going to get pureed!" she whispered. "That means smooshed up like an eggplant."

Chuckie tugged at Tommy's sleeve. "Did you hear that?" he yelled over the noise of the cheering customers. "That man just said your daddy is going into the ring with the big meanie. Oh, Tommy, he's doomed, doomed!" wailed Chuckie.

"No, he's not," said Tommy. "'Cause we're gonna save him. I gots an idea!"

"I was afraid you were gonna say that," gulped Chuckie.

Chapter 4

Back at the Pickleses' house, Chas and Howard carried in the TV while Stu walked Grandpa Lou to the door. "Dad and Lulu can't baby-sit tonight," he reported. "I forgot it was their Dinosaurs of Disco dancing lesson night."

"What are we going to do?" asked Howard with dismay.

"We'll have to take the kids with us," said Stu.

"Gee," said Chas. "I don't think the mothers would approve of the kids going to a wrestling match."

"Sure they would," said Stu brightly. "First of all, the kids are too young to know what's going on. And second of all . . ."—he thought about a second of all—"second of all, they'll never find out! Anybody see the clicker, by the way?" He started pulling up couch cushions and feeling around for it.

The babies were in their playpen, listening to what the grown-ups were talking about. "Tommy?" said Chuckie. "How are you going to save your daddy from the big meanie?"

"All we gots to do is to get that big meanie back inside the TV where he came from!" Tommy said.

"We?" asked Chuckie, swallowing hard.

"But how, Tommy?" asked Phil.

"Well, my daddy uses this thing to make things on the television go away and come back again," replied Tommy. He pulled his diaper away from his tummy, rummaged around inside, and pulled something out of it.

It was the TV clicker.

"Wow!" said all the babies.

"What is that?" asked Kimi.

"It's a kicker," said Tommy. "If I point it at the big meanie and press the button, it'll kick him back inside the TV. I see my daddy do it all the time. He points it at the TV and the little peoples go away. Then he presses it again and they come back. It depends on what button I press."

"How do you know which one to press?" asked Lil.

"He could get even biggerer if you press the wrong one!" added Phil.

"This arrow goes down," said Tommy,

pointing at the VOLUME button. "I think it will make him littler."

Chuckie's eyes opened wide. "But ... but that means that we gots to go *with* the daddies to the big, scary playpen place!"

"That's right, Chuckie," said Tommy firmly. "A baby's gotta do what a baby's gotta do."

"Don't worry, Chuckie," said Kimi. "I know the meanies look scary, but Tommy will make them go back into the TV."

Just then there was a *beep beep* from outside.

"That must be the limo!" cried Howard.

Stu glanced out the window. "Huh? I've never seen a limo like that. All I see is a rusty old van from Reliance Appliance Giants. I'll go see what's going on." He hurried outside. As Chas and Howard began packing up diaper bags Stu came back inside. "The driver says that the limousine is in the shop," he explained. "But he says there's plenty of room for us and the kids in the van."

The dads scooped up the babies and headed for the door. "You kids are in for a treat!" said Stu excitedly. "When you see these big guys parade by in person, they really knock your socks off!"

Chuckie closed his eyes and sighed.

Chapter 5

"Thanks for the ride," said Stu to the driver as the van pulled up in front of the arena. The dads unloaded the babies, strollers, and diaper bags. Dil had fallen asleep in his car seat.

The driver leaned out of his window. "I gotta go pick up a few barely used appliances from the junkyard," he said. "I'll come getcha after da match." The van rattled away.

Throngs of people were heading into the huge stadium. Inside, music boomed. Cameras flashed. Spotlights swooped across the sea of people.

"Oh, my!" shouted Chas, looking around. "It's certainly loud in here!"

Kimi sat up high in her stroller, straining to see everything she could. Chuckie covered his ears and clung to his father's neck.

"How about these seats!" shouted Stu. They had arrived at a row of empty seats directly in front of the ring. A padded railing was all that separated them from the wrestling area. "They weren't kidding when they said front row, huh?"

"If we lean way over to one side, we can see right around the cameraman," agreed Howard.

"Well, there's always the TV up there we can watch," bellowed Stu, pointing at the large screen suspended over the crowd. "This is going to be some wrestling match!"

Chas was looking around uneasily. There were people holding up big signs that said PULVERIZE 'EM! and others who had painted their faces. Practically everyone was yelling.

"Do you think it's safe?" shouted Chas, looking worried.

"We'll put the kids under this railing," said Howard. "They'll be safe under there!"

Dil stayed asleep the entire time despite the roar of the crowd.

"Tommy, did you see that big playpen?" Kimi asked.

"Yeah," Tommy said. "I heard my daddy call it a resting mat."

"Maybe the two growed-ups see who can take the longest nap," said Chuckie.

Just then the babies heard a commotion in the aisle next to them. A large man wearing a Viking outfit was being carried out on a stretcher.

"See?" said Chuckie. "He must be the best rester."

"Maybe that's why they're all so grumpy and yelly," suggested Lil. "They all need to take a nap."

The announcer was revving up the crowd, announcing the next match. "Next up, Knock-out Norman versus The Dude! Get ready for some seeeeerious action! The Dude says he's going to kick it up a notch tonight! Maybe he's learned a move or two from his food processor! What's it gonna be? Grind? Chop? Puree? Or Pulverize?!!!"

The crowd erupted into cheers as smoke began billowing down from the ceiling.

"Here he comes!" Stu shouted to Chas. "They should be calling me to the ring right after this match!"

"Gee," said Chas, as he noticed a man sitting on the other side of Howard whose hair was shaved into the form of a letter *D* for Dude. "I wonder what the moms would think of our being here."

Chapter 6

"I wonder how the kids are doing," Didi was saying to Betty and Kira as they stood outside of the Lipschitz conference room during the coffee break.

"Aw, I'm sure the fellas have everything shipshape," said Betty heartily, helping herself to several sandwiches that had been laid out for the mothers.

"I'm sure Chas is probably reading Kimi and Chuckie a nice bedtime story right now," said Kira with a smile. "I guess it's too late to call to say good night," she sighed.

"I thought Dr. Lipschitz was very persuasive in his last lecture," said Didi. "I'm interested to hear what he says in this next one." She looked down at her brochure and read, "'Television: Why Not Just Poison Your Child?'"

The mothers filed back into the conference room.

*   *   *

"What's going on, Tommy?" asked Chuckie, his eyes wide. While the dads weren't paying attention Tommy had climbed up onto Phil and Lil's shoulders. He could just see over the railing.

"Well, the big meanie that excaped from the TV is huggin' another big guy," Tommy reported. "And he just did a slumbersault and bounced offa the side

47

of the playpen. And now the other growed-up is standin' on top of the playpen ropes. That doesn't look too safe. And now he just jumped down right on top of the other big meanie. There's a growed-up with a stripey shirt who keeps blowin' a whistle. He looks a little scareded. Maybe he's trying to keep them awake 'cause it isn't time to rest yet."

"What are they doing now?" asked Kimi.

"Now the other guy is finally takin' his nap," Tommy reported. "The guy in the stripey shirt is bangin' on the floor next to his ear, tryin' to wake him up, but he looks like he won the resting con- test."

"I sometimes get grumpy afore *my* nap too," Lil admitted.

"Me too," said Phil, as he struggled to

keep Tommy steady. "And I'm grumpy right now."

"Now the man with the mikeyphone is standin' in the big playpen next to the big meanie that escaped from the TV set," said Tommy. "They're holding each other's hand. Now they've raised one arm up over their heads, still holdin' hands. They must be bestest friends."

"The match is over!" Stu shouted excitedly. "They're going to call my name next!"

Tommy huddled in close to his friends. "They're gonna call my daddy's name!" he said. "He's going to go into the ring with that big meanie! Get ready to roll, you guys!"

"Before we get to the next match, ladies and gentlemen," the announcer bellowed, "I am pleased to announce the winner of the One-Millionth Customer contest, sponsored by Reliance Appliance Giants. The winner gets to come into the ring with The Dude himself! Put your hands together for Mr. Stu Pickles!"

The crowd whooped and cheered. The music swelled. The Dude stood stock still in the ring, his arms crossed over his huge chest, scowling at the crowd. The babies watched in horror as Tommy's dad stood up and headed for the aisle.

Suddenly a man appeared at Stu's elbow. He was wearing a shiny suit and had slicked-back hair. "Vince Vanguard," he said, thrusting out his hand. "I'm The Dude's publicist. We'll just need you to slip this on so we can gain some exposure for his food processor during this publicity appearance."

He handed Stu a T-shirt. The writing said: I BOUGHT THE DUDE'S FOOD PROCESSOR AT

RELIANCE APPLIANCE GIANTS (WHERE RELIANCE IS PRACTICALLY THEIR MIDDLE NAME!) in big, bold letters. "Here are T-shirts for your friends as well," he said, and tossed them to Chas and Howard. Then he led Stu toward the ring.

Tommy waited until Chas and Howard were pulling their T-shirts over their heads. Then he motioned to the babies.

"Let's roll," Tommy said. "Gimme a boots, you guys." Phil and Lil heaved Tommy up and into the ring, and Kimi followed right after him. Then Tommy and Kimi pulled the others up and in.

The Dude took a step toward Stu. "How ya doin'?" he said with a grin as several cameramen swarmed around. He clapped Stu so hard on the back Stu stumbled forward. Then The Dude grabbed him around the neck in a

friendly headlock. The crowd cheered and whistled.

"Hey!" shouted Vince Vanguard. "Where did those babies come from!" He yanked a cell phone out from inside of his jacket and began to punch in some numbers. "Does The Dude have a new baby angle in his act that I haven't been informed of?" he bellowed into the phone.

The Dude looked down in surprise at the babies. He loosened his grip on Stu, who fell to the mat and bounced gently a couple of times.

Tommy wasted no time. He pulled the clicker out of his diaper and pointed it at The Dude. Frantically he pressed the VOLUME DOWN button as The Dude approached.

Chapter 7

Back in their seats Chas and Howard clapped and cheered along with the rest of the arena, although they were unable to see around the cameraman. But then the cameraman stepped to one side.

"CHUCKIE! KIMI!" Chas's voice could be heard above the roar of the crowd.

"PHIL! LIL!" Howard yelled at practically the same moment. He hopped into the ring, breaking free of security.

Chas managed to crawl through the stomping feet of frenzied wrestling fans and stoop under the ropes of the ring. He set down the baby seat cradling sleeping Dil and opened his arms. "Chuckie! Kimi!"

"Tommy?" Stu said in a muffled voice from where he lay slumped on the mat. "How did you get up here?"

The Dude grinned at the babies. He took a step toward them and in one quick swoop, picked up all five of them in his tree trunk-sized arms. "These your young 'uns?" he asked the three dads.

Stu rasied one finger. "Yes, sir. Yes, they are."

"Well, I think they oughtta be on TV too, don't you?" asked The Dude. "Come on, all of us together."

"Whatever you say, Mr. Dude," said Howard.

The Dude, the dads, and the babies were paraded around the stadium on a victory float.

The cameramen began filming from all angles, as the crowd roared. The Dude planted a loud kiss on each baby's cheek.

*   *   *

An hour into his seminar about television, Dr. Lipschitz discussed the perils of prime time. "If you can beleef it," he said in his thick, Eastern European accent, "there are actually mothers out there who permit their children to observe this sort of thing on de TV! Observe!" He walked over to the large television set and pointed the remote at it. The wrestling channel flashed on. Cameras were panning over a sea of frenzied wrestling fans.

Didi leaned toward Kira and Betty.

I BOUGHT
THE DUDE'S FOOD
PROCESSOR AT
RELIANCE
APPLIANCE GIANTS
(WHERE RELIANCE
IS PRACTICALLY THEIR
MIDDLE NAME!)

"Can you imagine?" she whispered, shaking her head. "What sort of parent would . . ."

Suddenly the image of The Dude appeared on the screen, holding the babies in his muscular embrace. Next to him, grinning and waving at the camera, stood Stu, Howard, and Chas.

"AHHHHHHHH!" shrieked all three mothers at the same time.

* * *

The announcer was going wild. "I don't be-LEEEVE it!" he shrieked. "Who would have known The Dude would have such a *soft* side to him, huh?"

The crowd let out a collective "Awww."

The Dude grinned at the dads and handed over the babies. "I gotta run," he said to them. "I'm supposed to be

backstage for a TV commercial. Take care of these cuties, wouldja?"

There was a popping sound, and then a blast of purple smoke billowed down from the ceiling, setting the fathers and babies coughing. When they opened their eyes, The Dude was gone.

"See?" said Tommy happily to the others. "Did you hear him say he was going back into the TV again? It workeded!"

Chapter 8

At the end of the evening the van was outside the arena waiting for them, just as the driver had promised.

"Gee, they really *are* reliable, aren't they? . . ." Stu's voice trailed off as he saw Kira, Didi, and Betty standing in front of the van, their arms crossed.

"Uh-oh," said the dads at the same time. "We're in trouble."

*　　*　　*

A few days later the babies and their parents were back at Buck E. Bee's restaurant. Tommy and Dil were flinging balls around the ball pit. Chuckie and Kimi were pretending to have a wrestling match between Chuckie's toy, Reptar and Kimi's toy, Superthing. Both toys were lying on the floor, covered with blankets, resting. Phil and Lil were sitting in front of the wall of televisions.

"Look, you guys!" called Phil. "It's the big meanie!"

Sure enough, twenty-five identical images of The Dude flashed in unison. He was holding up a bottle of lotion with dainty lilacs on the label. He grinned awkwardly at the camera, revealing several gaps in his teeth. "Even tough dudes like me need a little pampering sometimes," he growled. "Try this. It'll make

your skin as soft as a baby's. I should know. I love babies." The commercial cut to a clip of The Dude planting a kiss on Tommy's forehead.

Then the Reptar program came back on.

"The big meanie's back inside the TV where he belongs," Tommy said. "But what am I doin' in there?!"